This book belongs to:

Sophia

Printed in the United States of America

First Printing, 2016

ISBN: 978-0-9862176-2-3

Manufactured by Thomson-Shore, Dexter, MI (USA); RMA140JM42, November, 2016

To children everywhere
who remember to
think kindly of others.

A Story of Tall Tales

by Kerry Patterson

Illustrated by David Habben

Meet Kate Hales—she's seven (nearly eight),

thoroughly pleasant, and totally great.

And just what's so great about little Miss Hales?

She refuses
to tell

The tales Kate avoids DON'T involve a brave hero
who battles five dragons and fights till there's zero.

They're also NOT about knights
who wrestle with monsters
in spite of the bites.

The tales Kate rejects are the thoughts we all THINK
when others do stuff that makes our life stink.

HERE'S HOW IT WORKS

Kate has two older brothers, Curtis and Nate.
They both tell

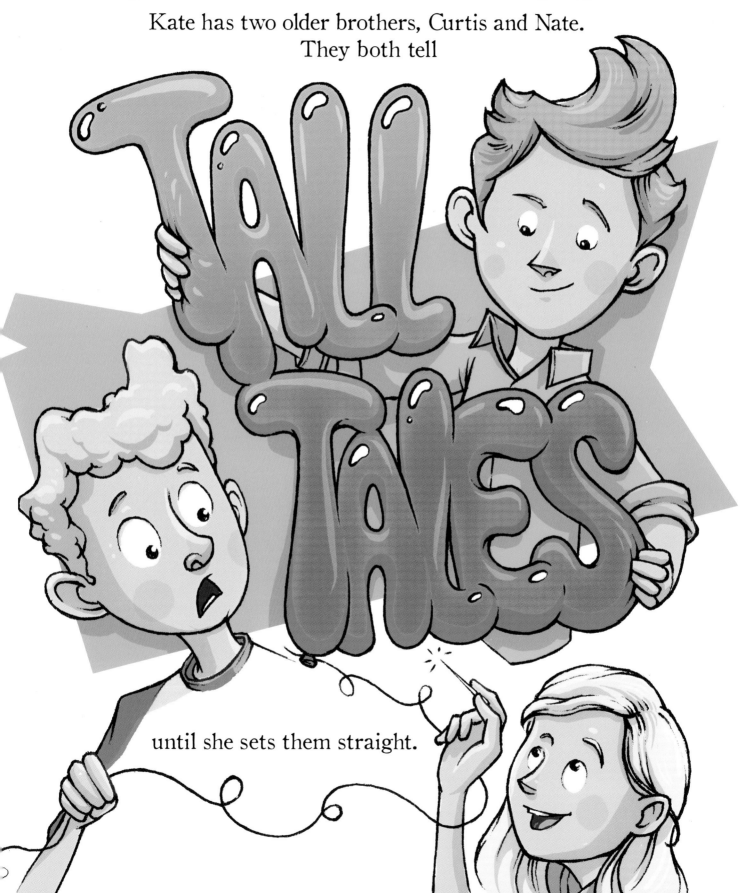

until she sets them straight.

FOR EXAMPLE

Curt builds a spaceship
that's simply terrific
out of **whatnots**
and
gizmos
and
things
nonspecific.

It has lasers and blasters
and razor-sharp wings…
'cause these are a few of his
favorite things.

One day Curt returns from playing next door
and finds his prized ship in a wreck on the floor.

It sits in a pile of ten billion bits,
like a giant just crushed it with TEN MILLION HITS!

Nearby lies a toy spinner. It's Nate's and looks new,
except for some dents from a bite or a chew.

Curt spots the toy and thinks: "IT'S A CLUE!"

"He hit my ship with a powerful blow,
first with his toy and then
his big toe—just for show.

"Wait till Mom learns of his despicable ways!
She'll ground Nate forever—plus seventeen days!"

Next, Nate and Kate walk through the door.
Curt grabs Nate by the collar and shouts with a roar:

"Not me!" shouts Nate.
"I bet it was…
…hmmm…
let me think.
Who messes things up and
makes our life stink?"

"I know!" Nate continues, "I bet it was KATE
and her gymnastics gyrations—there's little debate.
She attempted a difficult double back-flip...
and crashed on top of your wonderful ship."

"I agree!" says Curt. "I'm sure it was Kate.
As sure as I was when I thought it was Nate!"

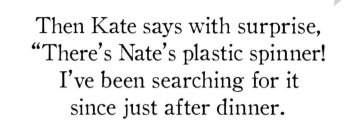

Then Kate says with surprise,
"There's Nate's plastic spinner!
I've been searching for it
since just after dinner.

"Our dog Skip grabbed it—that silly old hound—
then ran into the house and dashed all around.

"So who do you think ruined the ship?
Was it me? Was it Nate?
Or do you think it was Skip?"

"But, Curt, you were sure that Nate did the wrecking.
And then, Nate, you blamed me without even checking!"

"Your inflation," says Kate,
"is filled with big whoppers,
fat lies, bad assumptions,
and fancy showstoppers.

"What starts out as a story

ends up a tall tale.

What starts out as a minnow

ends up a giant whale."

"I can't picture," says Curt, "a world without stories about wizards, and knights, and all of their glories."

"If we can't talk," says Nate, "about vampire tombs, we might as well sit and pout in our rooms."

"You can tell stories," Kate politely explains, "about muscular heroes and monster remains. But don't tell tall tales about your brother and me and all of the other people you see."

What does KATE TEACH US?

When you don't know who broke the spaceship you built
and you wonder who should carry the guilt...

Stop inventing and telling outrageous tall tales.

Don't Turn Small Minnows into Giant Blue Whales!

Author's Note

Sometimes the people around you act in ways that cause you problems. For example, you've been sitting in your dentist's waiting room for nearly an hour because your friend hasn't picked you up yet. What's up with that? Or a coworker fails to help out on a particularly grungy job. Or (if you're a kid) maybe your brother wrecks the terrific spaceship you just built. (Well, you're pretty sure it's your brother who ruined it—who else would do such a thing?)

In each of these cases, if you don't rein in your imagination, you're likely to start making up reasons that explain why others have disappointed you. If you're like most people, the reasons you invent can be accusatory. You jump right over the harmless notion that your friend simply forgot to pick you up or that your coworker was pulled away to a different job. Instead, you assume the worst of others because you're convinced that they don't care about you. In fact, you're pretty sure they actually enjoy causing you problems because they're inherently mean and selfish. In short, you're the victim, they're the villains, and there's nothing you can do about it.

Except for one thing. You can make up the reasons behind others' actions. That is, you can make up a story about what they did and why. Some of the story elements you come up with may be correct—but when you act as if your fabrication is completely true, it can get you in trouble.

For the sake of this children's book, we'll call the inventive, and often inaccurate, stories humans come up with to explain others' actions "tall tales." We'll suggest that it's okay to read and tell stories about monsters, mummies, and the like. The same is true for sagas and legends about heroes and dragons. But it's not acceptable to tell tall tales that speak ill of real people, particularly when the stories are based on details that are a product of one's own fertile, and often biased, imagination.

To teach this concept to children, we've created Curt, a nine-year-old boy who builds a cool spaceship. Sadly, when he leaves his room, someone or something destroys it. When Curt returns and finds his masterpiece in ruins, he immediately assumes that his older brother, Nate, did it because, he tells himself, "It's just the kind of thing my creepy brother would do!"

Then, not only does Curt assume Nate is guilty, he also makes up several unflattering and totally wrong details to explain the event. As Curt's tall tale grows, he ultimately treats it as true and hurls a false accusation. Nate responds to being blamed by blaming his younger sister, Kate, and making up his own story. Fortunately, Kate (the hero of this story) comes in and sets things straight. It turns out that their dog broke the ship. All of this takes place because Curt and Nate transform small details into a tall tale—and in so doing, turn a minnow into a whale.

Kerry Patterson

Kerry Patterson has coauthored award-winning training programs and four *New York Times* bestselling business and self-improvement books. Recently, he has focused his writing on sharing memories and life lessons with his children and grandchildren—first in a memoir called *The Gray Fedora: Lessons on Life, Business, and Everything in Between* and then in books for children, including *It's Never Too Late to Be Nice* and *The Great Zooberry Debacle*.

David Habben

David Habben is an award-winning illustrator based in Salt Lake City, Utah. He and his family live in the shadow of the Wasatch Mountains, where they enjoy the company of wonderful friends and family. To see more of his work, visit him online at habbenink.com.

Also available from

PATTER 🐾 TALES

It's Never Too Late
to Be Nice

This illustrated children's book invites the reader into the Kingdom of Yabbit—a fanciful place that suffers terribly from a revenge ethic until a boy named Indy breaks the cycle.

The Great
Zooberry Debacle

In this book, the reader encounters a zany zoo that just might fall to bits unless its plucky young heroine can teach the animals and zookeepers alike the value of teamwork.

Visit us at
www.pattertales.com